RURAL ROUTE #1

NOT ALL GHOST STORIES ARE FAKE

ASHLEY KAMMERAAD ZUIDEMA

ISBN: 978-1-969463-34-1

This book is dedicated to my dearest friend Tonya.
Who always believed in me and my writing.
I love you, girl!

TABLE OF CONTENTS

INTRODUCTION

Enter into a world where not all ghost stories are fake. This book contains short stories, which will have you on the edge of your seat with each page turn. Each story is based on events that took place after the mother passed away in my previous novel *Dear Mom... It's Me... I Miss You...* from sinking floors to ghostly conversations, each chapter is a story in itself. Don't miss this one-of-a-kind story to share with others.

THE HOUSE

Short Story 1

My home is rich with warmth, but a dark gloom of a cloud folds overhead. The windows and doors are covered in dark blinds. There is no sun to move through to light my way. The sun is crested through one large window in the front of the house. Its bright rays light the family room like a welcoming hug from an old friend. However, brief that a hug may be. Walking past the icy cold linoleum floor to the soft rich carpet into the rest of the house is where this house story begins. Walking through each area of the house even the rooms have their own story to tell. Each room is different than the next in terms of the size, space, color of the walls, to the location of the windows and their coverings. The vibe of each room is a delicate part of the story that the house is trying to tell me. It is fair to say that their stories are ever changing much like the house.

Moving here has always felt like a mistake. It doesn't feel like home to me. This house feels like a distant stranger you are never able to adapt to having around. A stranger that decides my fate. A stranger that should have been protecting me, instead of making things more difficult for me. Someone who guides and loves you. Is this home really a friend or foe? How comfortable and safe do I feel here?

I have always felt like a home is supposed to be someplace that you feel comfortable in, free to make choices, learn valuable lessons in life. A home is somewhere you are happy and full of life. A home is where I am supposed to feel loved and wanted. Not here, not now. This place feels strange to me. It is not inviting and has an eerie vibe. The house sits on ten acres and is surrounded by woods. I often wonder what has happened in this place before I moved in.

How many families lived here before I did? What happened to them? Did anyone die here, or born?

The sense of emptiness looms in the air despite the stuff surrounding me. Having space can be an issue for some. The more space I have the more stuff I acquire to fill my space. What void are we trying to fill by adding more stuff? Are we missing something or trying to fill a need? Is it something we are missing in life or love? What happens to the stuff when we leave this place?

The trees surrounding the house speak to me as you walk around the property. Their limbs swaying in a gentle breeze, left to right, right to left. As if with each movement they are telling a story of their own. Standing outside in the quiet country air, natural life talks to you. If I listen carefully, the whisper of their branches, *"Get out... Get out..."* With one big whoosh the word *"NOW."* Comes with a cold wind from the leaves. Then I feel it, the tingle up my spine, the feeling of a presence that was not there before, the tickle on the back of my neck like a soft gentle touch, the goose bumps form along my skin, and you question... did I hear that right?

In this house I wait and wonder. What is going to come next? What will the house tell me tomorrow? Each day the story is different. It is this house that leads me in my decisions for the day. Feeling adventurous or wanting to stand still, the choices are endless but finding that listening will tell you everything. The air surrounding the house is thick with pine, maple, grass, and moss. The trees are thick, and their years are ever apparent by the thick base. These trees were here long before I was and will be here long after I leave. The smaller trees have a long life ahead of them and I am sure they only hope not to get cut down. Their roots penetrate deep into the ground. They have made this place their home and wish to keep it that way.

A small utility shed sits next to the house. Reminds me of a small cabin in the woods. It has the country look all over it. The doors and walls are made of wood. There is a metal latch on the front of the doors. It is the misplaced lock that absolutely does not fit in and has no business being there. This shed is a home for many different things, both alive and not. Its inhabitants have multiple legs and sleep in different areas. I will need to look closely before walking in. If

I am quiet and listen long enough, they will speak to me and tell me whereabouts they are. To ensure that they respect my space and I respect theirs.

The freshly built pole barn is a vast playland of things to do. The big metal doors facing the front and rear of the property is a never-ending roller coaster of ins and outs. The racetrack surrounding the doors and barn is a continuous circle for a kid on their bike or even running. In one door and out the next and starting all over again on completion of the first circle. Dodging stretched out tree limbs from smacking me in the face almost in warning to stop before I get hurt, like a mother tree protecting her saplings from flying too far away. The wood stairs leading to the loft area overlooking the whole barn is always a sight to see. The amount of stuff that one individual can put into a place is baffling. Will all this stuff be used? I have my doubts. The pole barn is built within a section of trees between the house and the neighbors. They do not seem to mind so much.

I often find myself sitting in the back yard, looking out past the brushes and wondering what is out there. The four acres behind the house has always screamed danger. Danger of walking past that safety line. The line that determines where I feel safe. Having that determination in my mind to either sink or swim. It is up to me to decide what direction I choose to go. Looking beyond that line everything seems fine and safe, but what I do not know is the quicksand underneath my feet, my life will be sucked into the abyss of those that have been there before me. Did they make the same mistake I did? Did they cross the line thinking that they would be safe also, but ended up sinking further down? Did they call for help like I did? Knowing full well that no one would hear them. The house heard me, but cannot save me or stop me from further sinking in.

Taking a step back, turning and facing the house. I walk back toward the front of the house. I know right now I am safe. I choose not to cross the line. Not today. Today, I choose me and my life. I never know what tomorrow will bring. Will the day be full of adventures through the house, finding a haunting memory I would rather ignore, or will the abyss behind the line call me? Not today, maybe not even tomorrow, but one day this house will be the last place I will call home.

THE KITCHEN FROM HELL

Walking into the house, the first area I arrived at is the kitchen. It sits facing the back of the house, but the blinds are drawn to block out the light, creating a dark and eerie entry to the house. The kitchen is smaller than it looks.

The kitchen cabinets are brown wood with a black trim inlaid in the cabinet design. The trim around each cabinet is shaped like a shield. A shield is like a warning to all those entering, *you shall not pass*. The handles on the cabinet doors are metal with leaf shapes on each end and are almost black in color. The color of the wood, trim, and handles matches the dark and eerie feeling of the house.

Standing in the kitchen, there is a distinct feeling of pain and suffering. The fading light that streams through the room slowly casts an ominous shadow on the refrigerator and stove that sits across from the window. Walking past the stove towards the refrigerator, a sudden pain in my right-side. Grasping my side, slightly leaning to the right, I look around, wondering what I ran into or what hit me.

The ominous glow is now surrounding the refrigerator. Already in pain, I slowly move closer. The fridge is out of place in this house. A plain cream/beige color that does not fit into the wood vibe.

Releasing one hand from my side, I reach for the refrigerator handle and open it. Replacing my hand back to my side, in an instant, the door suddenly slammed shut. Baffled, I reached for the handle again to open the door. Hesitation hits, thinking twice about reaching for the door, I can't help but wonder. You open it again and take a step back.

The door slams shut harder this time. The refrigerator shakes when the door hits its frame. I suddenly hear a soft cry, *"Stop it, that hurts, stop it!"* My head whips around to see where that was coming from.

In a fog of clear gray smoke, I see someone on their knees with part of their body in the refrigerator door. Out of shock, I took a step back, and the door was slightly open with the light streaming out of the side. There is a man standing over them with his hand on the door. It suddenly slams shut again, and I hear it again. The sobbing to please stop. Repeatedly, the door opens and slams shut. The man speaks enough to say, *"You don't need it, get out."*

Slowly, the person on their knees makes their way out of the horrendous slamming of the door. Crying on the floor, they crawl to the edge of the floor to the carpet. Standing on their feet, I can now see it was a girl. The next assumption is that the person doing the slamming was this poor girl's father. She is hunched over in pain, hands over her right side, walking back down the hall. Turning to look at the man once more, the gray smoke lifts, and the man is gone. Realizing that I was holding my breath this entire time, I am finally able to exhale from the experience.

Just as I turn to walk past the refrigerator, I see the gray fog fill the room once more. I froze in place. The image of the same man and a woman stands before me. Yelling fills the air; it is muffled and hard to make out. The man stands close to the woman, uncomfortably close as he continues to yell, and I notice that one of his hands starts to raise. The woman takes a step back, and he lowers it. The image on her face displays fear, anger, and hatred at the same time. Her eyes are squinting as she looks at this man. She stands taller than he, but not by much. It is hard to believe that the man could intimidate this woman.

Out of the hallway, another individual walks out with hands flailing and yelling. A phrase close to *"If you dare hit her, you will have to go through me."* It was the same girl who was slammed in the refrigerator door before. This time she is taller and a little older. She steps in between them, using her body weight to push him away from her. The man steps back, and he knows he has gone too far. He retreats to the chair in the kitchen and sits, holding his hateful expression. The girl and the woman walk away into different parts of the rest of the house. The gray smoke lifts one more time, and with no hesitation, I attempt to make my way out of this abusive kitchen that reeks with hurt, pain, suffering, fighting, arguing, and a blanket of lies with little love.

As I turn to move toward the carpet, I realize that I can't move. I tried to move my feet, but they are stuck to the floor, as if they were glued. As I attempt one more time to pull my feet up to move forward, I hear the sole of your shoe beginning to rip and pull apart. In a moment, a sheer panic began to set in, and the more I tried to move, the quicker it sank me in. My heart begins to race as the panic of never getting out of here starts to wash over you.

Quickly starting to look around, searching for something to grab or someone to help. Knowing that I am the only one there, it is up to me to save myself. The look of fear captivates my face, and panic begins to set in. My heart begins to race. I feel the beat of my heart throughout your whole body. Thump, thump, thump. A fear of being stuck in this house forever, lost to the world and everyone you love, dying in this house that was once a home, I knew it is now or never. I must get out of this house.

Trying repeatedly, I pull and tug to get out of being stuck. My shoes begin to move slightly with each attempted pull. Panic continues to engulf my whole body. After what I have seen, I do not want to be stuck in this world, I know I need to get out. Scraping against the wall and counter, I calmed down enough to break free.

Upon freedom, I fall forward onto the carpet ahead of me. The feeling of freedom engulfs my body. Trying to catch my breath... I look back... It can't be... There is no possible way... Am I losing my mind? What happened… I know what I saw, felt, and heard. The feeling of astonishment and anger fills my body like a wave crashing at the sea.

Looking back, the floor is as normal as it was when you first walked through the door. It was then that I knew that it had got me. The house has got me. It has got my mind playing tricks on me, seeing things, and believing in things I never knew existed.

Shaking it off, I knew I must keep moving, I know that the house has many more stories to tell me, and the one room that you want to avoid at all costs is next to enter. The room of the dead has its own story it needs to tell me, although I really want to avoid it. But I moved on.

THE ROOM OF THE DEAD

Just to the left of the kitchen is the room of the dead, just ten steps away. There is another door to the left of the arches of the room. Once again, the door is a dark brown wood frame with a series of splines going horizontally down the center of it. At first glance it is just a door, a seemingly simple closet door. The darkness behind it sends shivers down my spine. Behind the door lies a reflection of white and glossy eyes watching my every move.

The conduit into the room is like a tunnel into another atmosphere. The room leaves nothing to the imagination. An icy chill runs down my spine as I stand at the gate. What happened in this room to create such a spine-chilling feeling upon entering? At first glance, the room appears to be a normal everyday living room. The energy in the room is horrifying. Trying to take the first step into the room, I am immediately pushed back by a strong force. The wind is like a hurricane blowing me off my own two feet. Shaking off the eerie sensation, I try one more time. Pushing through the wind, like I am trying to push through a tightly woven spider web. Clawing and ripping, I finally make it through. On the other side, I realize I have stepped into another dimension.

The moonlight casts its shadow into the empty rectangular room. I need to squint my eyes to see through the darkness and shadows of the outside world coming through. The room is vacant, shadows dancing on the walls in the moonlight. It is dark, I need to move slowly.

The interior design of the room is light in color. The carpet on the floor is an off-white opaque with hints of gray. The walls are white, almost too white, and bare. The large windows at the center of the far wall allow those to see out and everyone and everything to see in. It is a terrifying feeling.

In the blink of an eye, the darkness is gone, and a low, soft orange hue is cast over, and I enter a dissociative state of mind. The true trauma of this room comes into light. All at once, I feel the sensation of being in tears, then anger consumes my body, and as I begin to look around, I see it. I understand that the room is trying to tell you what happened here. A rush of cold and fear overwhelms me. There, in the corner near the front entry door, it sits. The cold slab of a gatch bed. An imprint where a person's body lay is centered in the cushion on the slab. The cold metal of the clinking metallic skeletal rails squeals with agitation with every motion. The crisp white sheets reek of death, sickness, and bleach. The stench is overpowering, consuming my nostrils, causing my eyes to begin to burn and water. I try to turn it away and wipe it away, but it won't stop.

Out of the corner of my eye, I catch a glimpse of something I had not seen before. The blurry images of people appear around the gatch bed. I can see their expressions, sadness, and white invisible tears washing over their faces. Their voices are muffled; and it is difficult to grasp what they are saying. Many of them do not move. They are just standing there huddling together around a kitchen table. The area where you stand is clearly visible from the other room. My mind begins to race, and I begin to think to myself, *Can they see me?* The smaller of the shadows stands near the doorway. Standing frozen, looking, I see one begin to move. I nervously go into fight-or-flight mode, unsure if I should stay or move. I am frozen where I stand, my feet refuse to move. The shadow enters the room and kneels at the edge of the cold frame. Reaching forward and grabbing the empty sheet, the shadow's shoulders begin to shake violently, and a puddle of dark, clear, wetness begins to spread over the side of the sheet.

It is then that it hits me like a bolt of lightning out of a thunderous sky, that someone has recently died in this house, and I am standing in the aftermath. Standing frozen, watching the shadows, the orange-yellow hue of the light begins to fade, and once more the cold blackness surrounds you. An overwhelming pressure of grief hits me like a wave crashing against a stone sea wall. Falling to my knees, I began to cry. Crying not because I am sad, but because of the overwhelming emotion coming from within.

With a horrible feeling of dread, I begin to resume my stance. My body feels heavy and limp. Each step taken feels like such a heavy, daunting task, but I know that I need to move forward. The fear of being swallowed whole in the darkness, I move slowly toward the door frame. Out of the corner of my eye, to the right, I catch a glimpse of a tall gray shadow in the corner of the room. As fear once again washes over me, gathering all my strength, I dive through the door frame. The soft light of the kitchen washes over me like a warm sunrise. Feeling relieved and scared at the same time, I begin to wonder what the rest of the house has in store for me. I hope I can make it through.

INTO THE BLUE

The amount of sadness this house radiates with it is devastating. The hurt that so many have gone through and still made it out alive. Every house has its own story to tell, and this one has many stories to reveal.

Leaving the room of the dead, I barely have the energy or strength to keep moving. I move heavily about the house, down the hallway, to the first room on the left, a room that is half blue and half white. It is an interesting palette. Blue can symbolize various concepts: coldness, depression, sadness, and detachment.

The paint is rough. Running my hand down the walls, it pierces the skin on my fingers, leaving a small mark of blood on the wall. At first, it seems like it is nothing, but before I know it, there is more blood, way more than what my finger could produce.

I stand back, stunned as the blood drips down the wall. It started as a small smudge on the wall and started to drip thicker, darker, and heavier. Where was all this blood coming from? I look down at my finger, and there is a tiny scratch, not enough to produce the amount of blood on this wall. I return my eyes to the wall, and the blood has vanished, just as it appeared; there are no marks, stains, or spots of its presence, the little spot my finger has left vacated its claim.

I turn to continue to look around the room. It was empty, but a strange presence maintained its claim. The hairs on the back of my neck were standing on end, cold chills ran down my spine, and I knew then that I was not alone in this room. A feeling of dread, sudden feelings of sadness, and fear creeped under my skin. I started walking toward the middle of the room and suddenly hit something. I looked down: a queen-size bed appeared in the corner. I took a step back, a girl was sitting on the bed, shaking, crying, and rocking herself back and forth. I wanted to go to her and comfort her, ask her if she was okay, hold her like a mother holds her child. I knew that she would not see or hear me, so I stayed standing where I was.

The same man who was in the kitchen prior had entered the room. I was fearful of what I might see next. He walked over to the bed, and the girl's head shot up, eyes glazed over from her tears. She raised her hands to protect her face, but at that moment, the man's right hand came down and hit her right on the head. She began crying hysterically, yelling, "*Daddy, stop. Daddy, stop.*" The more she cried, the more her father hit her repeatedly. He said to her, "*If you are going to cry, I will give you something to cry about.*"

The girl looked right at me, like she knew I was there. Shocked, I stared back at her. I wanted to help her, but I knew that was impossible. The man looked around, as if he was looking to see what she was looking at. He huffed and stormed out of the room. The look in the girl's eyes almost felt like she was relieved he had left, but deep down, I knew that he would be back.

I was right, he came back into the room like a blazing fire, fueled by oxygen. In his right hand, he had his black leather belt. He grabbed hold of the left end of it, spread the center out, opened it, and snapped it right in front of the girl's face. He said to her, "*Why do you make me do this? Why can't you just be a good little girl?*" He raised his hand up in the air, the belt hanging from his white fingered grip. His face red with anger, hands shaking, and before I knew it, the girl screamed out with pain when the belt hit her on the side of her face. She wailed in pain, crying, screaming, hunching over, holding her face.

Her left hand had slipped under the pillow as she held her face with her right hand. She had turned and looked right at me. This time I knew... She knew I was here... My mouth wide open, eyes staring, unable to turn away, I saw the glint of silver slide from under her pillow. She had a knife. She looked at me again; this time, she had a smirk on her face. It was almost as if she had planned this. Did she know I had been in this house the entire time? What on earth was she going to do with it? I shook my head at her, mouthing "No!" She looked right at me and mouthed, "*You know you want me to do this...*" Like a flash of lightning, she rose onto her knees and raised the knife to her throat. The father stood back, dropped the belt, and looked at her. She looked at him right in his eye; there was no life left in her eyes. She knew she needed to stop this abuse before he killed her.

He said to her, "*What are you doing?*"

She said to him, "*I will cut my own throat if you lay one more hand on me... If you really want me dead that much, let's just get it over with right now.*"

He said to her, "*I do not want you dead. I want you to learn.*"

She began to slowly dig the knife deep into her throat. A small sliver of blood began to drip down her throat to her chest.

She said to him, "*I could kill myself right now, and everyone will believe you did it. Everyone knows what you do to me. They will just think you went too far.*"

He stood back, looked at her, and said nothing. I saw a tear creep in his eyes. He shook his head and walked out of the room.

Relief washed over both me and the girl in the room. She had won. She threw the knife to the floor and fell back onto the bed. She placed a washcloth over her cut and lay there, catching her breath, her chest rising and lowering with every breath she took. I looked at her and said, "*You knew I was here?*" She looked back at me and said, "*Yes, I have seen you in the house since you arrived.*" I did not respond, just stood there, breathing heavily, looking at her, watching the blood slowly stop dripping into her hair.

Her eyes closed, feeling at peace. She had cried all the tears she could, stood like a stone against the storm, and won the fight she had been fighting all her life. She looked at me one last time and whispered, "*Stay.*" I nodded my head as she fell into a deep, heavy sleep. I stood there watching her feeling at peace, while the room slowly disappeared before my eyes.

I was still not at ease with the situation, as I had walked out of the room and slowly closed the door behind me, locking all its dark secrets behind me.

THE WHITE ROOM

Stumbling away from the room of the dead, feeling completely exhausted, scared, but still curious at the same time. I decided to continue and make my way down a dark, narrow hallway. There is very little room to comfortably walk through. It feels like I am walking down a hallway of delusion, a tunnel that continues to get smaller as I continue to move forward.

Ouch! I feel a slight sting on my head, realizing my head is beginning to bang on the ceiling. I begin to feel anxious and unsure whether I should continue. I must slightly bend my knees, making it easier to walk while ducking my head. Straining my neck, I peer back down the hallway to the rest of the house as it disappears behind me. Standing alone, the end of the hallway feels so far away, and continues to get smaller as you go. The walls are shrinking into a small tunnel recoiling the doors with it. The walls begin to cave in on me.

Hesitantly and determined, I pushed on. The house has shown me many horrors, and I know that there is more it wants to tell me. There are four wooden doors along the corridor. On the right side of me is a door that leads into the bathroom. Curious, I look in. There are double-stacked linen cupboards behind the door. The cupboards in the bathroom are the same as in the kitchen, brown with a black shield outline on the front of them. Next to the cupboard is a shower bath along the left far wall and a toilet on the right with one sink. The countertop is littered with hairbrushes, hair ties, toothpaste, toothbrushes, makeup, a dryer, and a curling iron. I can tell that teenage girls use this bathroom. There is a small basket on the floor next to the toilet containing kids' bath toys. The space is small with enough room to stand alone in.

Backing out of the bathroom and heading further down the hallway, there are three rooms toward the end. To the left is a room with a blue wall, which is very out of the ordinary for a house that is filled with all white walls. At the end, on the right, is a room that has a wood-like floor and white walls.

The color of the third room is also white, unfavorable, and devoid of personal personality and life. The white carpet with gray hues matches the rest of the house. It does not look like it has been lived on, no footprints, no unraveling strings or edges, and no stains. Off-white vertical blinds cover the two windows in the room.

Did the house restore itself once its owners moved out? It is eerily clean and well-kept. Were the owners that OCD that the floor had to be always kept clean? Was someone too scared to get dirt on the floor? Why do I feel like I am not alone in this space? I feel like someone is standing next to me, but there is no one there.

Walking into the room, I continue to have the feeling that someone or something is watching over me. The hairs on the back of my neck stand on end. A cold chill runs down my back, and goosebumps begin to cover the skin of my arms. Apprehensive, I slowly turn around.

A distant sound of wind erupts from the entrance of the hallway, into the room, and a sudden rush of air comes blasting toward me, almost knocking me down. Gripping the door frame for life, the air rushes past into the room. The plain, bare, and bleak room begins to change, as it rolls over onto itself, like a fog rushing over the sea. This is a familiar experience I had in the room of the dead. The house wants to tell me something once again.

Refocusing my eyes, I look to the room once more, and a girl appears sitting on a bed. There are books and papers all around her. Her head is down, reading a thin book that lies in her lap. She has a pencil in one hand and a highlighter and a stack of papers in the other. The papers are swarming her as if trying to grab her attention to pick up each page, or afraid they are going to be missed. It looks like she is doing homework of some kind.

The bed looks small for a girl her age. Two medium-sized thin bed pillows are crunched at the top of the bed, and a faded, thin, Red Wings body pillow lies next to her. The comforter is brown plaid with blue, white, and teal stripes. There is a large white dresser along the far wall. It looks like it was painted to match the walls in the house. On the left side of the door frame sits an old-fashioned tube TV sitting on a black stand.

The television itself is black, small, and old. The screen is blurred out, keeping wandering eyes from noticing what is on. It is apparent that the girl is not paying attention to it anyway. The floor is scattered with children's toys and stuffed animals. Three small wooden tables, varying in size, stand next to the bed, surrounded by more toys. The top table has a light brown wooden lamp with a blue and gray striped shade. Next to the lamp is an alarm clock and a stack of both adult and children's books.

There are two windows in the room. Both are covered with white horizontal blinds. One along the wall to the right, where you can see the pole barn alongside the wooded shade of the house. The second window is on the far side and facing the front of the house. It is dark outside, and a storm is threatening to move through.

The wind begins to pick up outside. The shadows of the pine trees begin to dance along the walls of the room. The whispering sound of rain clattering on the metal pole barn outside the window fills the room and begins to dampen the noise coming from the TV. A bright flash of light shines through the window, then the loud electric lightning crashes with a thunderous boom and shakes the house. You can see the girl's body shaking like a terrified child. She looks up, but not at anything. She sits waiting and listening for the next boom to strike.

Rolling her eyes with an "oh, great" expression, she begins to shuffle around. She lightly tosses the highlighter into the center of the book. A handful of papers is put down on top of the book along with the pencil. She hastily shuffles the papers around her to one side. A long exhale comes from her mouth. Unwinding her legs she shifted over to the edge of the bed and began to rise to her feet. The light in the room is dim and soft white. There is very little light provided out in the hallway. She walks toward the door and into the hallway like she has done this many times before.

The dark, cavernous hallway is empty and void of any light or sound. The girl continues to walk toward the bathroom. She has her hands outstretched to the walls feeling her way along the path. Hesitantly and slowly moving one foot in front of the other.

Out of nowhere, she screeches, and, with a small thump, she stumbles backward to the floor, as if she ran into a wall. Lying on the floor like a spider fallen from its web. With eyes wide open, she looks up bewildered. Suddenly, another flash of lightning crashes outside and lights up the hallway through the surrounding windows.

At that moment, I see it. There, standing in front of her, is a large black shadow in the hallway. It says nothing and does not move. Just stands there looking with empty, beady, black eyes.

Petrified and unable to move, she sits for a second just staring into the dark in front of her. She opens her mouth to scream, but all that comes out is a silent shrieking. She moves to her feet as fast as her body lets her and sprints back into the room. Switching on the hall light, she looks down the hall. She stands shaking at the doorway with her hand on the switch, but there is nothing there. All I could hear was the rain smashing outside the window. Stunned and leaving the light on, she cautiously walks toward the bathroom door again. This time, she is moving at a slower pace. She peers down the lit hallway and walks to the bathroom, turns on the bathroom light and closes the door.

I stand there wondering what it was she walked into. Full of curiosity, I proceeded through the doorway and walked down the hallway. The chill bumps began to stretch over your skin again. I can feel the presence of something or someone, even though the hallway is lit up with a soft white light. I attempt to turn off the light switch, in hopes of recreating the events. I decided to walk in her same footsteps, as I tried again.

The thunder and lightning have stopped, and all that is left is total darkness. With arms outstretched, I walk on. There is a sudden drop in temperature. The air is colder than before and sends a shiver down my spine. Walking slowly down the hall, I pass the room with the blue wall. It is then that my fingertips feel something cold move forward briefly and retract in my direction. In fear, of the potential dark being in front of me, the shadow says nothing and does nothing as I walk backwards towards the room.

With my heart beating in my chest, radiating into a loud banging in your head and your ears, I grasp my chest and steady myself with one hand on the door frame, trying to catch my breath. Thinking to myself, what just happened? Did I just see a ghost? What was that? This house is full of horror and pain. You know that you must get out of here, but how?

The light turns on in the hallway again, I lift my head and see the girl walking back into the room and resuming her spot on the bed. Staring at her, I wonder... How did that just happen, and she does not notice. She begins to pick up her materials to start again, but she looks up at the door frame again. This time, she left the light on in the hallway. Too scared to turn it off, despite the late hour, and not caring who the light will keep awake. Stumbling to the doorway, I know I want to see the dark figure one last time, but my gut is telling me that this is a bad idea.

Reaching for the edge of the door, a small wind rushes you, it is gentle and warm this time. The hallway begins to fade around me. Looking back out of the corner of my eye, I see the girl is gone. The room is back to the empty space I walked into from the start. The house has shown me once more what it has up its sleeve. The question remains... What more does the house want to share...

EMERGING FROM THE SMOKE

After leaving the room of white, I could barely fathom the idea of taking one more step into this house. Every step I took, I felt a cold, tingling chill running down my spine. My skin felt cold and clammy, and I knew that what I had seen in the hallway had truly shaken me to my core. As the girl reentered the room, I knew then that it had shaken her, too.

I left the room and crept down the hall to the room next to it. It was a bare room, again devoid of life or color. The floor has wood paneling, white walls, and a ceiling fan with brown wings on it. The fan has an antique-looking base where the wings are attached by dark golden leaves. This room feels smaller than the rest. There is a small closet with dual swing-out panel doors, two windows, one to the right of the door looking out into the back yard, where you can view the pool, small deck, and the space between. The window on the left wall faces the side yard, where the big barn and row of pine trees are along the side of the house.

This room feels like a small prison cell, blank, cold, gray haze in the air, and stuffy. The lack of movement in the air makes it difficult to breathe. I started to cough, a deep, heavy, harsh cough. I looked around for the door, but I could not see past the smoke that had filled the room. It appeared like a dark fog out on a cold sea, rolling in off the shoreline.

I reached my hands out in front of me. I could barely see my fingertips. I moved slowly about the room, trying to feel my way around. A small vibration of wind had begun to circulate in the room. I looked up, and the brown wings on the fan started to swirl around. The gray smoke in the room began to lift into the fan, swirl around, and make its way to the opposite side of the room and down to the floor.

In the corner of the left side of the room, a large wooden desk with a white and blue office chair appeared. The desk was cluttered with papers, notes, books, and other miscellaneous stuff. To the right of it sat a short, small, narrow, brown filing cabinet with two drawers and a small, white office printer on top. I looked around the room and noticed there were guitars and cases along the wall behind the desk. On the left side of the room, against the wall, there was a full-sized bed with the headboard against the wall.

The bed was perfectly made. The corners were tucked in military style; the comforter was a dark blue with matching pillowcases. I turned my head to the desk and saw the father sitting in the chair, no clothes on, one hand on the mouse, and the other holding a cigarette. I was not sure what to make of this view, but I continued to watch. I noticed that the door was closed.

What was this man hiding? Why would he need to keep the door shut? I stood there, waiting, watching to see what would happen. It did not take long before I got my answer. The computer screen had come to life with a male and a woman having sex. There was a small chat in the corner of the screen. The man continued to smoke cigarette after cigarette, watching, and typing.

I realized now why the door was shut. The man continued to watch and type. I knew the girl had known I was in the house; is it possible that this man knows as well? I did not want to take the chance. There was a reason why this house was full of fear, and I understand why now.

There was a knock on the door, and a woman opened it. The man looked at her and closed out his screen. The volume was not on. She would have had no idea what he was looking at, or she already knew and did not care.

Their voices were inaudible as they spoke. The man was looking right at her and blew the smoke right into her face. I was surprised the woman continued to stand there and talk to him. I could tell that whatever it was he was saying to her had become heated. The man had this horrifying look on his face. He just stared her down, with his eyebrows raised, his head slightly tilted forward, his lips were pressed tight together, his face turning red. He quickly shot up, and the chair went flying past me to the corner of the bed. It slammed against the bed when the man walked to the door. He grabbed the door and slammed it in the woman's face. He grumbled to himself as he went back to the chair. He violently grabbed it, rolled it back to the desk, and exhaustively slammed himself back into the chair.

I was fearful that if I continued to stand here, I would be the next one this man would take his rage out against. The computer roared to life again. The man continued to type in the chat.

Curiosity had made me move closer to the computer. I walked lightly on my tiptoes, slowly inching my way forward. Just as I got close enough, the floor creaked under the pressure of my step. My body tensed up on the spot. The man turned in the chair to his right. I stopped, shoving my hands onto my face to silence any breathing, muffling any noise that may come through. Standing like a statue, I did not move.

The man looked around, never getting out of the chair. He shrugged and went on about his business. I took a deep breath of relief. I slowly took my last step closer to the computer. I could see the man was chatting with someone; her picture was placed on the side of the chat they were in. I could see she had long blonde hair, a thin face, a narrow nose, and what appeared to be full lips. The rest of her was not visible, but I could see where this was going. I started to read a little. I was instantly disgusted with the content.

Based on the conversation, it was apparent this man had some sort of relationship with this woman. I knew at that point that the man was hiding something. He had an internet lover, and the woman in the house had no idea. I had to leave this room. I turned quickly and walked to the door. I did not care if the floor made noise at this point. This jerk deserved whatever it was he was hiding, and whatever outcome that may come. I grabbed the door handle and pulled. The door swung open. Turning to look before I left, I could see the room had dissipated back into the hollow, empty shell it was. Shaking off the gross, I walked out and back into the hall. I knew that it was time to go. I had seen all this house wanted me to see. I knew I could not handle it anymore.

As if speaking to the wall, I thanked the house for allowing me to roam its walls and learn all the horrors it possessed. I said goodbye to the girl and wished her a happy crossover.

I made my way back down the hall, stopping at the room of the dead, crossed myself, and walked into the kitchen and out the door. Leaving everything behind me. I walked, consistently looking back to make sure no one or nothing was following me.

THE SPACE BETWEEN

The experience of the house so far has left haunting memories, not soon to be forgotten. I already know and understand that this house and property have unique qualities, and the average person would walk away from it. Some areas of the house have truly shaken me to my core. The disturbing images will haunt my dreams forever.

The countryside backyard sat peacefully, bathed in the afternoon sun. A long and wide field with shades of green and brown. The grass and weeds stood tall, towering over any onlooker attempting to cross their path. From the house to this section of the yard is stunningly mowed with cut marks showing the line where the powerful mower grazed the grass in one fluid motion.

The mower lines stop dead in their tracks at the edge of the field; not one blade of grass along the line is bent out of place, not one footprint has ever dented this perfect view. The ground is dark, wet, and mushy, like a spring melt has cast its dew in the ground. Standing at the edge of the space between the house and the field is like tempting to enter a corn maze. It is tempting to go in, but the overbearing stalks plant my feet where they stand. I want to walk forward to see what, if anything, lies ahead of me.

Hesitation settles into the core of my stomach, comparable to a heavy wave crashing to the shore. The empty space in front of me taunts me to wade out into its outstretched palms. Unknowingly, my left foot slowly rises to take my first step. At that moment, it hits me, a dark shadow of doubt questioning my next decision. The heel of my foot quickly returns to the spot it began. The questions start to race through my mind…

What-ifs start racing through my mind. What if I get stuck in a hole? What happens if I walk out there and get hurt? No one is around or will hear me scream for help. A slight breeze begins to blow; the trees begin to wake and sway. Gently, stretching their limbs as if waking up for the first time.

Making the decision to move forward, with each step, the sounds of scratching, cracking, and snapping echo through the air. The small, dry, overgrown weeds and branches below your feet ache with each step forward. Making my way through the thick, overgrown brush beyond the manicured lawn. A gnawing pain begins to creep up my arms, and looking down, I see that they are covered in scratch marks that are beginning to bleed. Shaking it off, I continue to move forward.

It's quiet out here, almost too quiet. The trees rustle around me, and there are small noises from animals scurrying around in the open space. Glancing back, I realize I have gone further than I thought. The ball in my stomach begins to drop, and I question whether I should keep going or turn back. There is so much to see out here, and I want to see more.

Just as you begin to pivot my feet to move forward, I hear something. Not the sound of small animals, but something different. The echo of a small child's voice can be heard in the distance, as if someone is yelling out to me from the yard. At first, it is distant and mumbled. With my eyes squinting, I try to see, but no one is there to be seen.

Deciding it was nothing but my imagination, I decided to move forward. After a few steps, it comes again, a small voice lingering in the blowing breeze. Turning again to see if anyone was there, but still no one. Near the middle of the field, I notice that there is a small clearing. It appears out of place in the middle of the field, almost as if the empty space was made there on purpose.

The space is square in shape, void of any of the dry weeds surrounding it. The dirt covering the top is fresh and not dried out like the rest of the field. The grass on top is green and evenly spread. The idea of a grave lurks in your head. Trying to move closer to get a better look, a sudden wave of cold and nausea hits me, stomach turning, body shaking, not knowing what is happening, knees buckling under me as I collapse to the ground. A violent jolt of fear hits me, realizing I am out here all by myself, sick, and alone, bent over in this field where no one can see or hear me. Panic began to set in; this is what I was afraid was going to happen.

Out of nowhere, the noise is heard again. This time it is louder and more distinctive than before. A short, steady breeze blows through, and I hear the words... *"GET OUT! GET OUT!"* The fear has me crumpled to the ground. The words keep repeating through the wind. My eyes dart around, looking for the source of the echo, when out of the corner of my eye, I see it.

A gestalt shadow appears standing over me at the edge of the grave-like space. It is blacker than black and absorbs the surrounding light. It doesn't move, doesn't speak, with no face or distinguishing features, just stands there hovering over you.

Scared and confused, I decide to ask, "Who are you?" It says nothing, just points to the space in front of me. Its arm is cloaked in a transparent black robe that hangs from the body. There are no visible hands or fingers covered in the cloak of the stranger standing in front of me. Once again, the idea of a grave stirs in my mind and body. I have no intention of digging or trying to see what is buried here, if anything.

The question still lingers in my mind as to why this figure is pointing to that space, I ask it who it was. Is this person a ghost of someone buried here? Is it trying to tell me that I need to uncover a secret beyond the dirt? Is this supposed to be the last stand for me if you do not leave this place? Have I finally crossed that threshold between here and gone?

I knew better than to cross the line of the abyss that lay beyond that line. It called to me, and I sank into its depths. It is time to listen and get out of there now before **I am next**. Scrambling to my feet, I decided to make a run for it back to safety. The dried branches, grass, and straw sink as each foot hits the ground, scraping my ankles and legs.

Wondering if the figure is following me, I glance back and notice that it is gone. Just as I straighten out to face the house, something catches my foot, and I fall hard to the ground. Falling on the left side, I feel a stabbing pain in my hand and see that a stick has sliced through my finger. It hurts and bleeds, but I know I need to keep going. Getting back to my feet, I continued running toward the house. Like a fading moon, the figure falls farther away as I stepped closer back to the house.

The breeze starts to blow again, and the words *"GET OUT! GET OUT!"* echo once more. The breeze dies down as I finally reach the edge of safety. The echo has stopped, and the rich, lush grass feels like such a blessing to step on. Exhausted, crying, winded, and bleeding, devoid of energy and strength, I collapsed on the ground.

The nightmare of empty space is over, and I am free, free to live life the way I see fit, and not shadowed by the ghosts of your past. Free to be myself and learn from my own mistakes. Free to live my life without being in fear of what will happen next. Freedom has been the only thing that has ever mattered to me, free from the abuse, free from the thumb that crushed me inside and out. Free to be yourself... Be yourself!!

It has never felt better to be in that place once and for all!

THE WOODS

Leaving the house, I walked down the half-mile driveway. The house sits next to about two and a half acres of nothing but tall, leafy, wooded trees. There is a small section of the woods along the road that has a small opening in it. Driving by, looking to the right, the opening looks like the entrance of a Jeep trail.

The path was narrow, but open enough to get a vehicle down it. The trees were starting to overgrow the trail. From the trailhead, it was hard to distinguish how far the trail went. Walking in the woods felt like I was walking from a familiar world into a dark, transformative world of nature. The smell of natural air is all around me. The air smells earthy, the sunlight filters through the leaves, and the sounds of nature are all around me. I walked slowly deeper into the trail. As I walked, I felt eyes on me with each step. A slow wind started to sway the trees back and forth. The sunlight was starting to go in and out, creating shadows all around me. The quiet solitude was calming in comparison with the house.

Walking through the shadows of darkness, I stumbled upon a faded structure barely visible through the overgrown foliage. The exterior was dilapidated, with the roof sagging into the structure. The windows were cracked and falling apart. Cobwebs were hanging like tattered banners, revealing the point where time stood still and moved on. The foliage was growing into the shack, reclaiming its space once again. The outside of it was barely holding itself up with old, mildewed, shredded wood. The air around the shack was still and heavy, creating an eerie orb in the air of surrounding darkness.

As I began to walk closer, there was a smell of rot, decay, and musk. It penetrated my nose like a skunk spraying its prey. The back of my throat tightened, and I began to gag. I attempted to cover my nose, but it was too late. I leaned over and began to vomit.

I took a step back to recover. What was dying inside of this thing that made it smell so bad? I took off my sweater and wrapped it around my head like a bandanna to block out the smell.

I attempted to walk closer once more. I looked through one of the broken windows. There were cobwebs hanging on every surface as if to claim the space for themselves. The dust had accumulated so that the entire surface was covered at least an inch thick. The items that were abandoned and left behind became barely distinguishable. Except one thing...

I continued to walk around to where the door would have been, and I could not believe what I was seeing. On the dust-covered floor were clean footprints. I took a step into the entryway, remaining in the frame, just in case. The footprints were the size of a boot. They were too large for a woman. Along the left side of the wall, just in front of a window, sat a small desk. It was old, wooden. It looked like it belonged to the shack. The most disturbing thing about it was what was sitting on the top of it.

In the center of the desk was a pair of binoculars. They had no apparent reason to be there aside from someone using them to spy or bird watch. They sat resting in the center of the desk. I stepped a little closer and noticed that the dust had formed around them, untouched and clean.

I dared to take another step further and reached for them. They were green, heavy, and required me to use both hands to lift them. The two refracting telescopes were mounted side-by-side, pointing in the same direction. There was a black leather strap that was connected on each side, allowing someone to wrap it around their neck for easier transportation.

I lifted them in the direction that they were pointing and was shocked by what I saw. They pointed right to the backyard where the pool was behind the house. Someone had been sitting here and spying on the owners of the house, watching their every move. They were able to see who was coming and going in and out of the pool.

Puzzled, I put the binoculars back down where they sat. I wanted to make sure the orbs of the glass were placed right back where they belonged. I could tell whoever was here last would be back soon. The footprints on the ground had not been covered in dust, indicating the distance between visits.

I looked around to see if there was anything else that would lead to a clue as to who it was. There had been nothing. The shack had been abandoned, and everything left had a growing expiration date on it. Even the chair that sat by the desk was unused due to the crumbling of the wood from which it was made.

I decided to step out and see if there was anything more I could see. I walked around the shack, and the back side had holes of fading material that was once solid wood. I could also see where the roof had begun to fall into the back part of the shack. The desk was facing the opposite wall from which it was hanging.

Around the corner, next to the shack, I could see where someone had been smoking and leaving the cigarette butts in the dirt with a few beer bottle caps. I wondered if whoever it was that was here had been living here or just close enough to walk over. I had not seen any tire tracks as I had approached, nothing indicating that someone had driven here in any vehicle.

I had decided that I had seen enough. I walked slowly out back to the road. The wind had picked up a bit, and the trees had begun to sway angrily. I remembered the horrible sound of the howling that came before telling me to *"Get out!! Get out now!!"*

I quickly walked back towards the road, turning my head back and forth to make sure no one was watching me. I was about halfway out when I heard a large crack, snap, and thud. A tree had landed heavily on the shack behind me. I started to shake, thinking that could have been me: I was inside there not but minutes before that had happened. The shack was completely destroyed under the thick bark of the pine tree.

Shaking, I had decided I did not care to walk back and look at the damage up close. My breath was heavy, my legs sore, and I was still shaking when I made it to the road. I was so thankful to touch the pavement that I bent down to my knees and kissed it. My car had been parked along the side of the road the entire time. I shot up and made a run for it.

I swung open the car door quickly, sat down in the driver's seat, buckled in, and drove off. I did not look back. To this day, the adventure in The House haunts me in my sleep. I can only pray that whoever takes over this property does not have the same luck as those in its history. *Fin*

ABOUT THE AUTHOR

Mother & Wife, Life-long learner, Educator, and Author. Ashley was born and raised in Holland, MI. Over the last 15 years, she has utilized her passion for education and learning. Ashley has obtained two Masters degrees—one from Baker College in Business, and the other from Grand Valley State University in Education. Ashley works from home as a Data Analyst and Researcher. She enjoys her freedom to write while working from home.

Ashley enjoys reading, crafting/journal making, and loves animals. Ashley has a German Shepherd (Ace) who loves to play frisbee in the backyard and go for walks. Ashley is a summer girl; she loves being outside in the sun, out on her boat, and off-roading with her Jeep Wrangler.

Ashley's mission is to empower women to take chances, fulfill their dreams, and understand that there is so much more to life than we could have ever imagined. She is determined to be successful at whatever she does and takes pride in her hardworking nature.

Ashley is currently working on multiple projects; a magazine specializing in where women write and what inspires their creative niche, a how-to book on creating the perfect journal, and a murder/mystery/thriller. Stay tuned for further details on her amazing projects.

Share your ghostly stories with a review on Amazon
and enter into the world of AshleyAnnWrites.com
for more stories coming soon!

www.ingramcontent.com/pod-product-compliance
Lightning Source LLC
Chambersburg PA
CBHW061054050726
47592CB00004B/1681